Jasper R Monroe

The Origin of Man

Or, the early reforms. A tale of tails

Jasper R Monroe

The Origin of Man
Or, the early reforms. A tale of tails

ISBN/EAN: 9783337089115

Printed in Europe, USA, Canada, Australia, Japan

Cover: Foto ©Andreas Hilbeck / pixelio.de

More available books at **www.hansebooks.com**

—THE—

ORIGIN OF MAN,

:OR:

THE EARLY REFORMS

A TALE OF TAILS.

:BY:

J. R. MONROE, M. D.

Editor and Proprietor of the Seymour (Indiana) Times.

1881:

Seymour Times Print.

A TALE OF TAILS.

1.

In the dim vista of the past, says science,
   Our earth lay lost in fogs of aqueous vapor,
Whelmed in thick clouds that bid the sun defiance,
   Who could not pierce them with his 'powerfulest' taper:
The oceans boiled by earth's submerged appliance,
   While rains perpetual helped to cool and shape her :
In fact the red-hot earth lay in an ocean
Of boiling water in perpetual motion.

2.

And there were eons of intense turmoil,
   Tumultuous warfare betwixt fire and water,
Rains poured on melted lava, to recoil
   In hissing steam, expanding with dread slaughter
To cooling slag and crust of sand and soil—
   Perpetual motion and perpetual motor—
The fiery globe deluged with pouring rain,
By touch made steam and driven back again.

3.

With force appalling and with heat intense,
   Expanding, hissing, bellowing, rushing, roaring
To colder regions which at once condense
   The steam to sheets of water, which re-pouring
Upon the fiery globe to be hurled hence :—
   Thus heat and cold, each robbing, each restoring,
Maintained the conflict for some years—say billions,
And as it's guess work, add some scores of trillions.

4.

Because the more we know the more we doubt,
   Where knowledge ends commences speculation,
Yet scientists but grudgingly give out
   Their real convictions for our delectation ;
They leave us to surmise what they're about,
   Not caring for our ignorant approbation ;
They break up nature's seals and seem content
To read her records with but small comment.

15.

I am not now and never was a poet;
  I tell my story in straightforward prose;
I'm not above, nor very far below it.
  But speaking of my story, now here goes:
A real bard would never let you know it;
  But as I've said, I am not one of those;
I am not crazy more than half the time,
And seldom lie, or lead in prayer or rhyme.

16.

Your real poet is quite wild while writing:
  (Half mad-man is he ere a versifier;)
He feels a mania for rhyme-inditing;
  But when he sees his prettiest thoughts knocked higher
Than kite or cloud, while those he cuts go kiting,—
  He for the exigence of verse a liar,
A laughing stock—as big an ass as—
Why goes he back upon his own Pegasus?

17.

Not he; not he; by rhyme he sees perverted
  His 'carefulest' proverbs and his best ideas,
But from his mania he is not diverted;
  He thinks the world as big an ass as he is:
Whate'er comes uppermost, out it is blurted;
  He rhymes you as he runs; his only plea is,
That poetry has license and no law,
And that he wins who makes you te-he-ha,

18.

Or weep and wail, bite lip, or grinders gnash,
  Or any way become extravagant;
Even if so crazy that you count out cash
  And pay him for his fustian and his rant—
If you are thus enthused, he's "made a mash,"
  And reached a climax every poet can't,
For when you stir men till they pull their purses,
You've wrought a miracle, if done by verses.

19.

Speaking of miracles—is it not queer
  That none of them occur these latter days?
If we could have a new one of this year,
  Right in the day time, in the sun's broad blaze,
The scoffer would behold and quake with fear;—
  Let dead men come from graves, and 'twill amaze
And startle unbelievers who defy us,
And make them call on Moses and Elias,

20.

Whom they deny. A troop of sheeted dead,
　With eyeless sockets and in naked bones,
Poking about Chicago would strike dread,
　And fill that Sodom with dire shrieks and groans;
And then the news would like red wild-fire spread,
　For winds would speak, and "capable" be stones,
Tho quite incapable the Chicagoans,
Who, like brave Falstaff, would be bawling Poins!

21.

And straight the monster heathen, Ingersoll,
　Would fly for succor unto Joseph Cook,
Recant his slurs on Solomon and Saul,
　And swear that Moses wrote a truthful book;
And B. F. Underwood would quickly call
　Upon his holiness, the pope, and book
Himself an applicant to kiss that toe—
And I—what I should do I hardly know.

22.

But then the slanders on the just would cease,
　And the good ministers would be respected,
The infidel would join the church in peace,
　And Christ our savior be no more rejected:
The holy men should ask the lord to please
　Work *one late* miracle, but well connected
With those of old, to stun the unbeliever,
And vindicate the church and to relieve her

23.

And them of lies so hard to struggle under;
　And which the wicked, fertile to invent,
And fiendish to proclaim in voice of thunder,
　To the great scandal, loss and detriment
Of church and minister, so 'tis a wonder
　That men dare yet proclaim that Christ was sent
To die for us and be made a scape-goat,
And that they took his garments—vest and coat,

24.

And crucified him on the cruel cross,
　Between two thieves, he being Jehovah's son,
And likewise god himself, with power to toss
　The mountains in the sea: and that 'twas done
Because god loved the world and bore the loss
　Of his own offspring, so that every one
Might then "believe," be reborn and immersed,
And if he didn't, might go god-accursed.

25.

This is the gospel, preached almost in vain,
  Because the wicked are stiff-necked and proud,
And scoffers, like Voltaire and Thomas Paine,
  Unhung, proclaim their heresies aloud,
So when a holy minister doth rain
  A gospel shower upon a wicked crowd,
They mark him for detraction—lie him black,
Even while blest by the prayers he sends 'em back.

26.

So many wicked lies the bad invent
  Upon the ministers we love so well,
That christians view with comfort and content,
  The retributive justice found in hell :
And here I will relate, with your consent,
  A sample lie, such as they love to tell,
And claim they'd *prove*, did not the courts exclude
From witness stand the bible-hating brood.

27.

I say with your consent, not that I pander
  To public taste, with taint hereditary ;
But that I find my muse must needs meander,
  And will not march to order arbitrary :
She oft reminds me of a cross old gander,
  That waddles aimlessly all day, with "nary"
Distinct idea of what he wants to do ;
Now running at and now away from you.

28.

And so my muse, capricious and refractory,
  Cannot be curbed, but must have room to range,
And steal materials for her manufactory
  On every hand, invading every grange,
Protected by invulnerable phylactery,
  She poaches recklessly, nor is it strange,
For souls erst bound, that tyrant chains have broke,
And freedom gained, will no more bear the yoke.

29.

But I have hope of bringing her around,
  By cautious measures, which I will not mention,
To move o'er mystic prairie, mount and mound
  Where erst our sires, in rustic mass convention,
And with mock gravity and awe profound,
  Were wont to ruminate on tail retention,
Reformers voting it a bore, unlawful,
In gents quite odious and in ladies awful.

30.

They'd reached this boldness through much tribulation,
  And years of struggle, for the common herd
Held tails the handsomest things in all creation,
  And cutting off ridiculous and absurd:
But I must get back to that sad narration
  Without another sentence or a word;
For me to get confused and lost in fog
Is easier still than falling off a log.

31.

Wheel in a wheel, a story in a story;
  Both illy shaped and neither necessary;
But I am writing this for cash and glory,
  With preference for the cash, decided, very;
A bard wants something tangible before he
  Resolves to the unreal, or the airy
But let me from our apish sires' repose
Back to the tale told by the pastor's foes.

32.

But let me premise that the allegations
  I do deny, and to the alligators
I hurl defiance, be what may their stations;
  I take no stock at all in paison-haters,
And give small credence to their revelations;
  To say the best they are but "small potaters;"
But let us hear them; truth may come from liars,
And revelations now and then from fires.

33.

There was a husband married some three years,
  Who worked at night till after three o'clock;
A pious christian, serving god through fears:
  His wife a word of blasphemy would shock;
She sang in the church choir—was oft in tears;
  Was dutiful and happy in wedlock:
She loved her husband, pastor, church and god,
And mourned for nations gospel-starved abroad.

34.

To tell the truth, she was the secretary
  Of the Young Women's Foreign Tract Society;
A zealous worker for the heathen, very,
  In foreign lands,—she shipped a great variety
Of beads and bibles to the missionary,
  With psalms, essays and rituals to satiety.
Her home and field of labor, staid old Boston;
Her work, to plant her savior in Hindostan.

35.

Then she was hospitable and very pretty,   •
  And tho not rich, moved with the uppertendom ;
She fed the ministers of the whole city,   •
  And railed at Kneeland, Savage, Seaver, Mendum ;
She kept her husband poor, but had no pity
  For her poor neighbors and no help to lend 'em :
The foreign mission and her church and preacher
Were the chief idols of this pious creature.

·36.   •

And then this charming lady'had her hates ;
  She hated all the churches but her own ;
She heard her church's side in all debates,
  But to the other side was deaf as stone ;
The beggar girl was hustled from her gates,
  Nor would she throw a stranger dog a bone :
She had no mercy on her fallen sisters :
Her scowls at infidels were Spanish blisters.

'37.

Her husband had but small magnetic power,
  But he was sober, quiet, steady-going ;   •
He deemed his wife a rare exotic flower—
  A rose-bud in his bodouir ever blowing ;
Each smile of hers was as a summer shower
  That kept the tendrils of his passion growing ;
But her own tongue could have impeached her honor,
Or killed the wild mad love he lavished on her.

38.

Then he was unsuspecting, brave, confiding,
  And felt much flatterred by the past'ral visit,
Or when the parson took his wife out riding,
  He took it as a compliment exquisite,
Prompted by gratitude for his providing
  The good man's wearing gear. I ask, Why is it
That pious husbands ne'er suspect the parson ?—
But I must hurry with my tale of arson.

39.

Three hours before his usual time our Ben
  Was hurrying homeward through the silent street
To his true wife, who watched his coming, when
  A cup of tea with victual good to eat
She always sate before him.—Here my pen
  Will fail to paint the happy home retreat,—
The wife's warm welcome and the fragrant cup,
The cake, the kiss—but I will give it up.

40.

Perhaps 'tis well that fate so oft keeps hidden
    The great calamities that end our hopes,
But bears our bark on waves of joy till ridden
    Straight to the sworl where the dread maelstrom opes
Its foaming cauldron: we should feel forbidden
    To trust our anchorage to sandy ropes;
To bind our happiness with ropes of straw;
"To trust a woman, or a suit at law."

41.

Life is uncertain, so is woman's virtue,
    In presence of the villain's arts and wiles;
And a great lack of confidence won't hurt you;
    To build your castles with a woman's smiles
Is to live out of doors: the storms will search you;
    A frog spawns in your pool—the water riles;
Your turn your head—a bug wades in your tea!
But you drink on, nor sicken!—You don't see!

42.

And thus is ignorance bliss, your life a dream,
    With rosy time by romping pleasures chased;
Your faith-built bark sails on a rippling stream,
    And joy is crowned by confidence misplaced:
A stealthy cat laps in your crock of cream,
    But you detect no difference in the taste,
Nor dream, when sleep weighs down your weary lid,
That late a cobra in your nest lie hid!

43.

But to my tale of fire: Dark was the night,
    And Ben was hurrying home with eager heart,
When suddenly, just over on his right,
    A cry of fire caused him to halt and start;
Not far away a cloud of smoke and light
    Broke from a roof, and sudden as a dart
He flew toward it, where arrived he spied
A sickening sight, and terrors-truck he cried—

44.

"Help ho! help ho!—bring quick that ladder! ho!
    There swoons a woman in yon open window:
There! steady men! there! there!—support it so!
    I'll save her be she Jewess, negress, Hindoo;
Girls have been rescued thus ere now, we know,
    And what one man has done another can do.—
There, lady, gain your feet; you're safe from fire!
Why goodness gracious! is that you 'Mariar?'"

45.

"Come, come this way," the lady said, regaining
  Her foothold on the pave, and readjusting
Her scant attire, "and as 'tis wet and raining,
  Wrap me in your great coat, (you're true and trusting,)
And let us home, while I go on explaining
  The life I've led—a life grown so disgusting
That death by fire were almost a relief!—
But now I'll burst my bonds: Then to be brief—

46.

(And kill me if you will as I proceed)—
  That is a house of assignation, and
Your trusted pastor has a room there feed,
  Where I your wife have gone at his demand
Five nights in every week—so great his greed—
  For near three years—coerced, you understand,
In part at least, and coaxed and plied with vows,
And crazed in conflicts of lust's fierce carouse!

47.

Here seat you by our happy hearth and hear
  The horrid story!—speak not till I'm through; ·
I'll stir the fire and fix the supper near,
  ·And we'll talk calmly as we used to do;
Tho happiness will henceforth disappear
  From this our home, and peace from me and you,—"
She said on reaching their abode, and then
She calmly sat down by the blanched Ben.

48.

It happened thus:—the day that we were wed
  You were called off and kept all night away;
That night our pastor stole him to my bed,
  And played the bridegroom till the break of day;
My room was isolated, and he plead
  And forced the feats no female power could stay;
And this, too sore and wretched scarce to speak,
Is why I kept my sick bed near a week,

49.

And kept my lawful husband from his own—
  From the ripe harvest he so longed to reap,
Not knowing that blasts about his flowers had blown
  And stole their freshness while he lay asleep!
Nor dared I to my husband then make known
  Why I lay wakeful all the night to weep:
I dreaded that fruition would disclose
But withered leaves for tulip lip and rose.

50.

The puzzled doctor could not guess my case ;
   The pastor came with pious resignation,
With not a blush upon his clean-shaved face !
   He the cursed cause of my heart desolation !
Implored in my behalf the throne of grace !—
   And told me when alone my soul's salvation
Lay in concealment—that 'twas no more sin
To give my priest my person than a pin.

51.

And afterwards at greater length dwelt he
   Upon the subject of the pastoral call.
He said the christian wife was bound and free
   To yield to Christ her body, soul and all ;
And that the pastor is Christ's legatee,
   And consequently heir to what would fall
To Jesus were he here.—The church who weds
Takes Christ and pastor to her arms and beds.

52.

And to convince and make assurance sure,
   He cited scripture to back up his views,
He said that wiving with the priest was pure ;
   In olden times the priests all wives did use,
Yet had none of their own : in periods newer
   In claiming this the priests incur abuse ;
Housewives and pastors come to think it wise
To hide their amours from all earthly eyes.

53.

And with such arguments being daily plied,
   Is it a wonder I again did yield ?
I plead a little and a while denied,
   But soon gave full possession of the field ;
Nay more—the varied loves and games we tried
   Seemed more and more a witchery to wield !
So I became a slave to passion's power,
And writhed in ecstasy from hour to hour!

54.

Tho seeming cold, unyielding oft to you,
   When in forbidden fields I was all flame ;
You had one gait, while his was ever new ;
   His paces were all fury, yours all tame ;
You were so tender with me ; timid, too ;
   While he saw in me but a wanton dame,
Whose nature needed sturdy discipline,
And who once broke would bogle at no sin.

55.

Such dame, tho listless oft in lawful arms,
 And sleepily receiving legal tender,
When the debaucher revels in her charms,
 Glows with fierce fires that lust appears to lend her :
His neighbor's garden thus the man who farms
 Receives a harvest richer than 'twill render
To the proprietor by lawful tillage :
Thus love's best pearls are the product of pillage.

56.

I have no faith at all, my noble Ben,
 In women's power to parry the invader,
Especially as in my own case, when
 She's a young wife—a reverend the raider ;
She lends her lip to reverence, and then
 He raids by force, (when he cannot pursuade her
To yield it willingly,) her husband's casket,
Which once possessed is his whene'er he ask it.

57.

There is a certain novelty in sinning,
 That leads too many women on to ruin ;
After the first almost enforced beginning,
 There is a fascination in pursuin'
A game where all is loss—there is no winning
 A prize that pays a woman for wrong-doin' :
Yet once set wrong she ne'er regains her status,
But goes the downward grade for gain or gratis.

58.

You lords may stumble and regain your standing,
 But our first step from virtue's high estate
Involves a tumble to the lowest landing,
 Which our 'protectors' help precipitate ;
While our own sex is clamorous in demanding
 That we be left entirely to our fate ;
So our first fall is fatal for all time,
And what in you is 'cute' in *us* is crime !

59.

But recklessness is closely on the heels
 Of limping virtue, and in woman's liver
Oft lurk propensities that she reveals
 On opportunity that chance may give her ;
Her treachery she carefully conceals ;
 Her favors free as waters in a river :
Such specimens as this we sometimes meet :
Compounds of wantonness, falsehood, deceit,

60.

And then, a woman once resolved on throwing
    Herself away can fall a little lower
Then any creature else ; there is no knowing
    What trick, and scheme, and subterfuge, and more,
She will employ to keep herself still going
    Upon the lowermost plane, and to explore
The bogs and fens where hissing serpents crawl,
And tempt and taste the vices, one and all.

61.

To-night midst the revival's feverish heat,
    When our good pastor thrice in prayer had led,
He came and whispered to me in my seat
    That he'd escort me on my homeward tread ;
This is his custom. And to our retreat,
    Assuming our disguise in haste we sped ;
Disrobing me he still had on his clothes
When the alarm and cry of fire arose.

62.

He sought the door, the stairway was on fire ;
    He darted forth and left me to my fate ;
I got my shoes on—part of my attire,
    Then raised the sash—the distance, O how great !
I shudderingly drew back, keen my desire
    For rescue that my vengeance I could sate
Upon the wretch who could desert me so—
You came to rescue and the rest you know.

63.

I said I was disgusted thus to lead
    A life of fear, debauchery, deceit ;
But still I felt my savior's side did bleed,
    And that his blood would work out sin's defeat ;
But what digusted me was that the greed
    Of my destroyer led him late to meet
A little miss, late convert to his fold,
Oft in my bed if suffered to get cold

64.

From my forced absence :—think you strange of this ?
    Why I grew jealous where I ought to loathe ?
I can myself give no analysis
    Of the strange nature, origin and growth
Of jealousy that craves the Judas kiss
    While hating still the Judas—aye, that both
Loved and despised the mad, debauching bouts,
Yet reveled in them, with some halts and doubts :

65.

And that while weary of the spoiler's yoke,
  Would rather wear it than see it encase
A newer victim's neck, or have it broke
  Save by myself, and that to his disgrace
And deprivation:—But to thus provoke
  And shed me for a fresher piece of lace !
Filled me with scorn and *will* to dare the worst—
To raise the curtain and show him accursed.

66.

And then to-night his cowardly desertion,
  His sudden, cruel, and ungallant flight,
Without the slightest effort or exertion
  To take me with him as he could and might
And should have done—fed my new-formed aversion,
  And I there vowed, should I survive this night,
That I would straight this hypocrite unmask,
Confess my crime and your condonement ask.

67.

So now, dear Ben, I've laid my bosom bare,
  You know the worst, and now condone or kill ;
Speak man, or strike !—why blanch you thus and stare
  My life is forfeit, take it if you will ;
But do not kill me with that stony glare !
  Has your ear burst with horrors ? Hear you still ?
Are you struck daft ? Alas I blame you not :
This black recital should the sunlight blot !"

68.

Thus spoke the rescued, ruined wife midst tears
  And sobs that shook her finely-moulded form ;
But Ben, like one who neither sees nor hears,
  Sate like a statue in a blinding storm ;
Words seemed to take no meaing to his ears ;
  He held his hands out aimlessly to warm :
When suddenly a sickly, vacant smile o'erspread
His pallid face, and Ben fell back stone dead.

69.

They said it was the heat ; he'd swallowed flame
  In saving a bad woman at the fire ;
None noticed where she went, or knew her name.
  The poor wife shrieked for help in accents dire ;
The neighbors, horror-struck, in numbers came ;
  Shrieking, the wife fled forth in night attire ;
Pursued she was clear to the river's shore,
Where she sprang in and never was seen more !

70.

The pastor preached the funerals with great zest ;
 He said the lord, who doeth all things well,
Knew what for their departed friends was best :
 And that his ways were all inscrutable.
He said they were in heaven amongst the blest,
 He warned survivors of the pangs of hell ;
He said the dear ones who had gone before,
Through prayer would be rejoined on Canaan's shore.

71.

He said as without hope we should not mourn,
 But lean on Christ and lay our loads on him,
Who had a crown of thorns and thistles worn,
 That we might each become a cherubim ;
And that our burthens Christ had meekly borne,
 Indulging us and humoring every whim :
But that he cut our loved ones down to bring
Us hovering closer underneath his wing.

72.

He said that we should learn to kiss the rod ;
 We needed punishment for being allured,
By pleasures of this world away from god :
 And merriment and joy, he felt assured,
Midst which so many giddy people plod,
 Their downward way, was by our lord endured,
Because he is long-suffering.—Tears and gloom
Bring joy and happiness beyond the tomb.

73.

Laughter and merriment endanger souls ;
 All worldly pleasures god abominates ;
The theatre and the ball room are the shoals
 Where satan seins so many addlepates,
Hauling 'em in like fishes, to his coals ;—
 And circuses the lord intensely hates,
For there the clown, arrayed in gear fantastical,
Makes roars of laughter unecclesiastical.

74.

But wicked showmen, such as P. T. Barnum,
 To win the flocks, (no wickedness were worse,)
Send in free tickets to the parsons, (darn 'em !)
 And say the sacred cow and woolly horse,
And the behemoth very much consarn 'em ;
 And thus they rope 'em in, without remorse ;
But, clothed in heavenly armor, the bad clown
Evokes no sign from them, except a frown.

75.

Thus ministers are lured to the circu·ous
  ·By such device, and by the children's tears,
Where jokes three centuries old come rippling to us,
  And break-neck riders shake us up with fears;
And naked girls gymnastic, quite undo us;
  These last the parsons will not see, but cheers
From the vast multitude show that depravity
Is as potential as Sir Newton's gravity.

76.

The pastor closed with fervid exhortation
  Against the wickedness by satan planned ;
He urged solemnity and meditation
  Upon the awful change so near at hand :
He urged to penance, fast, prayer and privation,
  And thoughts all centered on that better land.
And then the sisters, each with weeping eye,
Came up to bid the dear good man good-bye.

77.

And'now I must to business in a hurry,
  And seek for vexed questions a solution.
About man's origin there's been much worry,
  Whether he came by god or evolution:
The scientists have caused no little flurry
  Within the church, that venerable institution.
The evidence afforded by the rocks,
The christian fable of creation knocks.

78.

And this at once removes the underpinning
  On which the christian church has been sustained,
And sends us farther back for a beginning—
  For knowledge which I fear will not be gained ;
I think I said, though you may call it sinning,
  How many ages water must have rained
Upon our fiery globe ere it contracted
And cooled to form a crust round it impacted.

79.

Obscured in cloud and smoke, cold rains descending,
  Upon its face vast oceans boiling hot,
With cold and heat continually contending,
  Our planet rolled for eons I name not,
But finally even of this there was an ending,
  And a beginning of low forms, I wot;
Gelatinous and quickened by the sun ;
And thus was life upon our globe begun.

80.

And steadily, as ages rolled away,
  Affinities were busy fixing forms,
But no man·god was forming them from clay ;
  Election and attraction—light which warms,
And hunger, which impels, were all at play :—
  Form grafted upon form, with helps and harms :
The weaker perishing to push the stronger ;   •
The less imperfect lasting still the longer.

81.

And vegitation in its myriad shapes,
  From water grasses up to giant trees,
Amidst whose foliage the ancestral apes
  Took refuge from devouring enemies,
Dining on barks and buds and nuts and grapes;
  Oft sung to sleep, in siege, by sighing breeze—
Was rank, but came not through *one* Great First Cause,
But through blind agencies, with loves and laws :—

82.

Absorption, motion, magnetism, change,
  The primal parents being heat and light,
And water, with its universal range,
  For which all forms have greedy appetite,
These were the builders; tho man thinks it strange
  That things can move without a moving "might,"
Outside of nature, yet throughout it still,
Creating, causing, governing through "one will."

83.

But I must sound my signal for "off brakes,"
  I must move faster o'er so long a road.
In the warm water of lagoons and lakes
  And seas and rivers anciently abode
Ungainly creatures, horrid-looking snakes,
  While jungles, plains and forests were well stowed
With beasts of prey ; and with such foes as these,
Our sires must serve for lunch or live in trees.

84.

For creatures of those times, not delicate,
  Had yet a relish for our long-tailed sires ;
In part from hunger, but still more from hate ;
  Because our fathers were such awful liars—
Now full of pranks most devilish, now sedate—
  So constant in that cunning which conspires
Against the quietude and peace of neighbors,
And so unceasing in nefarious labors.

85.

There is some guess work here, but then I shan't
  Without good reason any fact disclose :
Our sires had constant wars, their means were scant;
  And multitudinous their savage foes ;
They had few allies save the elephant,
  And he was grave and troubled with the "slows,"
But the čarniverous beasts and reptiles paid
Fear-born respect to this centurion grave.

86.

And so our sires were safer in his beats,
  As were all creatures, thirsting not for gore,
From the blood-thirsty brutes, devouring meats ;
  But so mischievous were our dads of yore,
That they must play their tricks and cunning feats
  On their protectors, who serenely bore
The slight annoyance from their friends at play,
But now and then slung one some yards away.

87.

Now I am crowding hard my Tale of Tails,
  And rushing for it like a train of freight ;
He knows no words like "faint," or "fail," or "fails,"
  Who will plod on and work and watch and wait :
The man who reads and at the writer rails,
  Is a galloot, a green-horned addlepate,
Who has no ear for a straightforward story,
And cares no copper for the author's glory.

88.

At first our parents were but polliwogs,
  Living at leisure in their warm lagoons,
Or bathed in sunlight, leaping like the frogs,
  Or climbing in trees, like catamounts, or 'coons ;
Their food the slime and insects in the bogs ;
  Packing to sleep when tired, like nests of spoons,—
With legs and feet, and arms and hands, and eyes,
And jumping power occasioning surprise.

89.

And they had ears for music and great throats,
  And held free concerts through the live-long night ;
But in such clamorous and discordant notes,
  As to appall the beasts, the reptiles fright ;
Thus, like the odor of polecats and goats,
  Their songs protected them, and put to flight
Their numerous enemies, with ears disgusted,
And every faculty worn out and "wusted."

90.

I am recording facts—at that epoch
  Our parents had no tails:—in this you'll read,
Although it may occasion you a shock,
  By jarring your conceptions, or your creed ;
But I won't our ancestral secrets lock,
  And tell you now in time, they felt the need
Of continuities like the opossum,
And cast about for means to make them blossom.

91.

Because at last they had been driven to trees,
  To 'scape the terrors of terrific claws,
And weak ones, losing holds in tops of these,
  Down came they in accordance with known laws;
And it would make their fellows' blood quite freeze
  To see them fall plump into open jaws
Of crouching lion, cat, or crocodile :
And yet such exit oft provoked a smile.

92.

So our ancestors, as I here have stated,
  Found that they needed anchors, so to speak ;
And where a want, to welfare near related,
  In any creature, be it strong or weak,
Has been long felt, and want on time has waited,
  That want has been supplied.—Nature will seek,
Where changed conditions call for special features,
To modify, engraft, and arm its creatures.

93.

With tails evolved our parents were secure,
  Lashed fast in tree tops, they could then defy
Their scowling foes, who hence had to endure,
  Their gibbering insolence as they passed by ;
But eons of evolving power, I'm sure,
  Were lost in furnishing this tail supply,
So they who wore them never did take note
That tails were not in vogue in times remote.

94.

Nor we of this day can peer in the past
  And note the time when the great change occurred—
When tailed men were talked of yet, and classed
  With creatures like ourselves : and change to bird
The loathed reptile :—processes too vast
  For our conception have all nature stirred,
For centuries where millions fail expression,
To bring the present status of progression.

95.

But let us be assured and note it well
   That creatures from which we must own descent,
In a dim era not discernable—
   Low forms crept upward, following still the bent
Of evolution, from albuminous cell,
   And by successive change, development,
Reaching at last perfection as we view it,—
What ups and downs! what struggles coming to it!

96.

But at that stage when men had long possessed
   Their caudal terminations does my tale,
Or should it open, if I had been blest
   With talent for narration—did not fail,
Through much perversity of rhyme, to wrest
   Dread secrets hidden by oblivion's vail,
And write them here on paper, like a man !
A thing I do not, nor believe I can !

97.

But let me to it :—Things had changed somewhat :
   Our parents had outgrown the savage creatures ;
They were as numerous as the leaves, and not
   The slaves they had been :—Talmages and Beechers
Had risen up, with intrigue, sham and plot ;
   And others with strange innovating features,
And so our fathers, having quelled their foes,
Found occupation as vexed questions rose.

98.

Many were noted for intrigue and sham,
   And shaved their fellows in a shameful way ;
And some were lecherous and cared not a damn
   Whose wives they had, as some care not to-day.
The multitude was curious, but to cram
   An innovation down their throats to stay,
Was a big job and hard on the reformers,
Who like our Talmages to-day, were "stormers."

99.

But jeers and gibberish, laughter and uproar
   Were mostly the poor ranter's sole reward,
When he denounced the usages of yore,
   And plead for something nearer in accord
With the progressive age—they called him "bore,"
   As sinners now call pleaders for the lord :
But agitation had progressed for ages
Before was reached opinion's turning stages.

100.

So it has been in later times; we find
    Long centuries wasted ere one step is taken ;
Inherited delusions making blind,
    And deaf and dumb, and error still unshaken
Upon its throne of prejudice, and mind
    Asleep in ignorance, slow to awaken
From its long slumber in the centuries,
And move to greener fields and sunnier skies.

101.

But agitation had developed thought,
    Which hard necessity had put to use ;
Just as it's doing to-day, and will and ought,
    For our perceptions are still quite obtuse,
In some regards, although we've surely wrought
    Some wonderful achievements—midst abuse
And opposition from the lord's annointed,
An opposition oftentimes quite pointed,

102.

And sometimes hot, for dungeon, sword and flame
    Have been the instruments, in godly hands,
To quell enquirers, make discoverers tame,
    And force obedience to divine commands.
The book of Genesis, a little lame,
    Was held to be sufficient, as it stands,
For man's requirements, and a further search
For information, was to butt the church.

103.

The earth was flat and rested on foundations,
    It had four corners, and the sun and moon
Were made to give it light, and their girations
    Were round and round it—such a heavenly boon !
And man to doubt, and start investigations !—
    No wonder they were burnt at stakes, and soon !—
The source of knowledge was the bible ope,
Yet some went poking with a telescope !

104.

But holy mother church made a good fight,
    And smote the innovators, hip and thigh ;
She kept her fagots burning day and night,
    But still enquirers seemed to multiply :
In course of time she had to flop, outright ;—
    The earth moved round the sun, none could deny :
Thence, fighting priests, discoverers plodded on,
Till Moses and his miracles were gone.

105.

But all of this took time, for evolution,
 Whether in matter or mind, is awful slow;
But slowly came the world to a solution
 Of mixed problems, and to see and know
Those truths, amongst the errors and confusion,
 That laid the faiths and superstitions low,
And led men to the umbrageous knowledge tree
Whose fruit has made them self-reliant—free.

106.

But dead across the investigator's path
 Hath stood the church—the clergy in all time;
Threatening the terrors of eternal wrath,
 And damning discovery as most heinous crime;
Whatever hate could do the clergy hath
 To kill reforms and bury truths sublime;—
The greatest blessings man enjoys to-day,
He's gained by holding church and god at bay.

107.

But to be just, and give the church its due,
 There's many vices it has bravely fought;
Its deeds of charity, not faint nor few,
 Have been with almost countless blessings fraught;
It has done something for good morals, too.
 And thousands of its votaries have sought,
And seek to-day to make their fellows better,
While binding them with superstition's fetter.

108.

So here I do them justice, as I should,
 Being without hate or prejudicial thrall,
But being opposed to shams, no mortal could
 Believe in Jonah, Jesus Christ, et al.;
Nor in the mother Mary's maidenhood;
 Nor the poor fable of old Adam's fall;
Nor in the father, holy ghost and son,—
One entity in three and three in one!

109.

Nor that belief in nonsense such as this,
 Is quite essential to eternal rest;
Nor that there is somewhere a hot abyss,
 Where some shall burn, while other some are blest,
Beyond this life; and that such happiness
 Is made to hang and turn upon the test
Of torture, penance and denial here,
With groan, and prayer, and sob, and sigh, and tear!

110.

All this I can't believe, nor will I try,
  It all is humbug, false pretense and sham ;
All come alike and all alike will die ;
  Nor can a priest assist to save or damn ;
He is as powerless as are you and I,
  To move the Fates ; and the alleged "I Am"
Is still more powerless—mythical, man-made—
Dream of a dream, shade of a shadow's shade !

111.

And so the priest, however much sincere,
  Is but a false pretender, preying on
The weaknesses, the trust, the hopes, the fears
  Of his frail fellows ; pointing to the dawn
Of immortality in other spheres,
  Of which he knows just nothing, but has drawn
His information from the misty past—
Fiction at first and falsehood to the last.

112.

It is immoral to deal in delusion ;
  To sell to ignorance what you do not own :—
Divine afflatus, unction, or affusion,
  To be effective in a world unknown :
And into happy homes how base the intrusion
  Of threats of endless fire, long face and groan !
Who deal in rights beyond this life are knaves,
And they who buy them are but stupid slaves.

113.

But ignorance is the essence of devotion ;
  It is the life and food of faith and fear ;
And priestcraft feeds on this devout emotion,
  And sells its pews in heaven for pennies here :
Who pays to priestcraft most has most promotion—
  Ascends the highest in the atmosphere :
Faith pays you nothing till you lose your breath :
You loan while living—you collect at death.

114.

But no one has come back to make report,
  How his investments and deposits "panned ;"
How if recorded in St. Peter's court
  He found his deeds to tracts of promised land :
He fought the good fight and he holds the fort :
  Crown on his head and harp within his hand .
He ought to have ; he *has* the preacher shouts ;
But he comes not to affirm, and we have doubts.

115.

But crowns or not, the priests secure their pay ;
  They sell the lands and send their flocks to find 'em :
Who must be satisfied, because they stay,
  And send not even a postal card behind 'em ;
Prancing, perhaps, the gold-paved streets all day ;
  All cables cut that to the earth could bind 'em ;
Surrendered wealth for god, or deemed as dross—
So cash accumulates about the cross.

116.

But I grow tedious, move too slow by half ;
  I'm trying to say discovery and invention,
That brought the telescope, type, telegraph,
  And several other things that I might mention,
By making longer this long paragraph,
  Have always roused the church's apprehension,
Lest Moses, David, Solomon might suffer,
Or be laid sprawling the last gospel duffer.

117.

And still I wander from our ancient sires,
  Just as I wandered from our fiery globe,
After the drenching rains, had quenched the fires,
  And nature had put on a floral robe ;
But if the patience of the reader tires,
  Let him recall how god afflicted Job ;
And let him choose between my rhyming diction .
And Job's sore boils, and other sad affliction.

118.

You see I'm running this for all that's in it ;
  My subject lost, I'm running with a looseness ;
Our planet's life and age and the infinite,
  Dread themes of mine, but deluged in "obtuseness,"
In consequence of cursed verse ;—to win it
  I drop my theme and lug in words whose "useness"
Is quite apparent ; but, a helpless man,
I'm doing now the very best I can.

119.

The preacher and the punster and the poet
  Find little comfort in this world of sorrow ;
They suffer, but they rather hide than show it ;
  They toil to-day but for abuse to-morrow ;
A kick feels good to them, because they know it
  Against the public weal—a work of horror
To build a pun, a poem or a church steeple
To undermine the morals of the people.

120.

But this digression from the fiery globe
  Is none of my own choosing, I assure you,
I'm working with the patience of a Job;
  And doing my level best again to lure you
Back to the molten era and to probe
  The secrets of world-growth, in hopes to cure you
Of notions into which the cloth betray us,
That it was made in just six days from chaos.

121.

I will get at it yet, if there is virtue
  In perseverence.—Oft some pounded ice
Placed on the caput, lest the strain should hurt you,
  When you grasp mighty thoughts, as in a vice,
And grind them in your brain pan—may divert you;
  By cold condensed to crystals in a trice,
Your thoughts may pour in gems from their brain crucible
Hence an ice-poultice is at times excusable.

122.

But I may get on without cold appliance;
  I'm not so hot as I am in a hurry;
I have to print the Times and hurl defiance
  At witches, gods and devils; and I worry
O'er my defense of ministers: so science
  Whene'er I make for her, appears to scurry
And scamper to elude me :—Goddess coy!
I'd woo you oftime had I less employ.

123.

But here I am at every object firing
  Except the one for which my guns were loaded;
The reader's patience and my time expiring :
  In fact, all parties near to frenzy goaded;
Who reads these lines will read without admiring;
  I suffer from this form of verse, and so did
Lord Byron, as you know, if you have read him,
Who, grumbling, followed where his stanza led him.

124.

But I am pinche'd a little more than Byron, he
  Was full of hate and did not care a curse,
So that the stanzas gave him room for irony
  He was not much inclined to make a "furse;"
While they the furnace of his spleen were firin' he
  Would let his stanzas wobble worse and worse,
With scarce a growl, but let them fall from satire!
Then he would make the pens and paper scatter!

125.

Nor could Lord B. abide a verse insipid;
  He wandered off where'er his stanza led,
But if it fell to tameness then he "dip-ped"
  His tongue in brandy, and in face grew red;
Then out a dozen oaths or more he "rip-ped,"
  Not fearing, as he should have done, Old Ned:
No stanza could play many freaks with Noel,
E'er he would grind it under his boot "so-el."

126.

But I'm some different, anyway, say "sorter;"
  I am inclined to grief and melancholy;
My stanza stumbling where it hadn't "orter,"
  Or dragging me to 'frivolousness' or folly,
Drives me not to hot brandy, but cold "warter,"
  In hydrant brought by system known as Holly:
And when I soak my liver through and through
I weep a little and again fall to.

127.

And then should my Pegasus run zig-zag,
  And cut up capers o'er my crucifixion,
And make me out a low-down scallawag,
  When I would show in dignified affliction,
Or paint me taking some grave reverend's tag;
  Or make my plainest facts appear as fiction—
Why, I don't kill Pegasus for these freaks:
I only lay my pencil down two weeks.

128.

There is a world of virtue in humility,
  And woes well husbanded are oft a blessing;
A widow turns her weeds to great utility,
  (But here again I find myself digressing,)
She laughs or cries with just the same facility—
  Sunshine and cloud alternate, keep you guessing
The color of her eyes, and whether to woo her
By wailing the old love or one some newer.

129.

But I go worse and worse the more I angle
  For incidents and ideas therefrom springing;
I have no wish upon the earth to tangle
  A woman up at this stage of my singing.
Though something further on I hope to mangle
  Those maids who tempt the minister, thus bringing
Reproach upon the church, besides some scandal,
And giving the infidel big clubs to handle.

130.

The infidel ! a name for one to loath !
   How can we tolerate the dreadful being !—
Denies our savior and his mother both !
   Nor with our holy church at all agreeing !
Denies the holy scriptures with an oath,   .
   And charges David, the good king, with spreeing !—
He also goes back on the holy ghost,
A thing that we could strike him for almost.

131.

And then he will dispute and even scoff,
   And the most sacred things will ridicule ;
In argument he heads the christian off,
   Exciting him, while he himself keeps cool ;
His hat to crucifix he scarce will doff ;
   In cussedness he almost beats the mule.
Of Sunday keeping he has scarce an "idy"—
And he eats flesh as well as fish on Friday !

132.

He will not dip his finger in the blood
   Drawn from the pierced side of dear Emanuel ;
He says no great deluge was Noah's flood,
   Nor were real lions in that den with "Danuel ;"
He tells you David danced without a dud ;
   He shocks and angers you, nor can you well
Forbear from lifting him on toe of boot,
And would if it were always safe to do't.

133.

But O, alack, the heavy day has come
   When laws *protecting* him are boldly framed !
Erst holy inquisition, screw for thumb,
   Throat clamp and fagot, the good christian claimed
With these he made the heretic succumb ;
   If not converted he was quickly tamed :
Dear gospel helps ! hid now in history's pages !—
No wonder that the hated heathen rages.

134.

No wonder he dares tell you that King David,
   Who was of our dear lord a distant sire,
Was a marauder, and that he beha-ved
   As a man-god should not, with one "Uriar ;"
As if it wasn't right, when the king cra-ved
   A subject's wife, to take her home and try her,
And if she pleased him well, to put the chattel
Where he would do most good—in front of battle

135.

Time was when king and priest could do no wrong;
    Then was the banner of the cross respected ;
The clanking chain, or flesh-imbedded thong,
    Thumb-screw, or rack, or skin from flesh dissected,
Or sluggish flame, reflected to prolong
    And show the goodness of the faith rejected,—
Then were the christian's aids badly needed,
To help the heretic believe as he did.

136.

The growth of doctrines not in scripture grounded,
    So dangerous to priests and potentates,
As that the earth, instead of flat is rounded,
    And that, instead of resting, it rotates,
(God's people and his precious book dumbfounded!)
    Should be by law suppressed in christian states :
And wretches who deny that Christ is god
Should be by legislative act outlawed.

137.

There is a science which they call geology, ·
    Relied on by some learned heretics,
To shake the corner stones of our theology ;
    They claim that this with Moses will not mix,
And that said Moses must make an apology
    For spending in world-making days but six ;
By glaciers, rocks, coal seams and certain strata,
They strive to overturn all bible data.

138.

Then the astronomers, so-called, attempt
    To prove god's footstool once a fiery ball :
God's own account should surely be exempt
    From contradiction, but not so at all ;
These star explorers swear that Moses dreampt
    His story of creation, and the fall,—
That worlds were formed by nebular contraction,
. And life by—something—say molecular action.

139.

For these irreverent savans avow,
    That there are other worlds besides our own,
And larger ones at that, but we allow
    If this were true and god desired it known,
That he would have revealed the fact somehow,
    And there is no such fact in scripture shown ;
Hence we conclude, and swear it on the bible,
That "Other Worlds than Ours" is but a libel,

140.

This, you will take it, is a fling at Proctor,
   A catholic whom holy mother shames,
Professing to revere her, he has knocked her
   "Flat of her back," with version of King James;
The cradle of the centuries has rocked her—
   He the first recreant to disprove her claims;
Still praising her, he mounts the platform, puffing,
And knocks from holy mother church the stuffing.

141.

But this they say he cannot help, for science
   Is the sworn enemy of revelation,
And Proctor, with his faith, has full reliance
   Upon the plain revealment of causation,
And tho he bids no deity defiance,
   He weakens on "world-making" and "creation:"
He turns his glass upon the regions stellar,
And thinks the bible god a dwarfish "feller."

142.

But other heathen, Darwin, Huxley, Haeckel,
   And such as they, god's darkest ways illumin'
The word of god they ravenously tackle,
   And swear men came from apes—they from albumen;
And like a flock of geese they strut and cackle,
   Pretending to great learning and accumen—
The working germ, the weaving bioplast,
They hold before you till you stand aghast;

143.

For you see nothing, and their protoplasm,
   Molecular selection and repulsion,
Electrified affinities, love-spasm,
   The missing link immured in an emulsion,—
(You strain to pierce the impenetrable chasm,)
   Throw you almost or quite into convulsion,
And you thank god that trust in him saves labor,
And inly hate your scientific neighbor.

144.

But these wise skeptics who raise doubts to tease us,
   Be-rack their brains and strain their microscopes,
To find their primal "cause."—It would displease us
   To find it lodged in matter—we're in hopes
To find redemption through the blood of Jesus,
   While broken are the skeptic's sandy ropes;
But he's remorseless—ravenous in research,
And may at last leave Jesus in the lurch.

145.

But should at last the sneaking scientist
  Prove false the record of our blessed Moses,
He should not have applause; he should be hissed!
  For then the citadel where faith reposes
Would be shook down; we could not then insist
  On god nor devil, and no one supposes
That the curs'd infidel who kills our friends,
Will give us anything to make amends.

146.

When we look round and see how fast are growing   '
  The dreadful theories of the wicked scoffer,
Who steals our hopes of heaven and hell, well knowing
  That he has nothing in their place to offer;
The seeds of fearful irreligion sowing,
  With not a word of "praise" or prayer to proffer
To priest or pope—for god no love nor awe—
We look again for solace to the law.

147.

The skeptic must be legally suppressed,
  God-fearing people be by law protected;
No christian must give any heathen rest,
  And he must be from christian hearths ejected.
The bible must be offered as a test
  At every poll where rulers are selected,
And only they must vote who kiss the book:
All others must be knocked, or kicked or shook.

148.

And god must be put in the constitution;
  And worship be enforced by legislation;
The war upon religion needs solution,
  Or it will quickly overrun the nation;
Already it is open revolution,
  With rebels delving under the foundation,
And mining to blow up beyond the moon
Our christian fabric—and they'll do it soon.

149.

The churches are dissolving all about us;
  The members stay at home, or sit and drink
Heretical discourses; and they scout us
  If we ask for the minister some chink;
They seem to tire of sermons, and they doubt us;
  They say they like the cause that makes 'em think,
For thinking, being the skeptic's occupation,
To the believer is a new sensation.

150.

And then our sabbath is being stolen away.
　Men desecrate it near our very doors ;
And if against such outrage we inveigh,
　You ought to hear the hated heathen's roars !
He'll swear 'tis just like any other day,
　And that he'll fiddle, ditch or do his chores,
Just as he would on Monday !—Holy ghost !
O give us back the good old whipping post !

151.

But O, unwisely have laws been repealed,
　And as unwisely other laws enacted.
Those that enforced god's word, to man revealed,
　And from the worldlian due respect exacted,
Have been destroyed, and christians have to yield ;
　So sacred canons are with scorn infracted :
There's nothing in the world will save us but
The old blue laws of old Connecticut.

152.

O, had we back again those wise decrees,
　With men to execute them as of yore,
How quick the infidel, upon his knees,
　Would grace and mercy of our lord implore !
Or if he didn't, him the law would seize,
　And put him where dogs would not bite him more,
Or we could banish, burn or mangle him,
Put out his eyes, or tear him limb from limb.

153.

Then worship of the lord would be enforced,
　Nor would god's holy day be desecrated,
Nor church and state be any more divorced,
　For the base infidel would be abated !
The heresies so learnedly discoursed,
　That man was evoluted, not created,
Would be unlawful, and all scriptural facts
Would be sustained by legislative acts.

154.

And that root of all heresies, called "science,"
　Would be dug up and cast into the fire,
For it and faith are never in alliance,
　And it makes god unlearned and a liar ;
Outlawed would be its books and its appliance ;
　For it is blasphemy in man to aspire
To any knowledge not in scripture bound,
For there sufficient for his wants is found.

155.

The telescopes, and wicked things what not,
  Retorts and crucibles, would be destroyed ;
Which, inconsistent with the polyglot,
  Most sadly have the christian world annoyed ;
All such appliances are hell-begot,—
  Against Jehovah are they all employed :
No telescope is pointed to the sky
That gives not Moses and our lord the lie !

156.

The impious whelps even steal god's agencies,
  They press his lightning to their uses base :
Whose is the imprisoned steam they use but his ?
  Where in the sacred book is there a place
Where god gives warrant for such work as this ?—
  This slavery of god's powers before his face !—
So science is at best but sacrilege
That steals god's subtle potencies to bridge·

157.

The skeptic's way across the hidden stream
  Where sleep the mysteries of the infinite,
On which through the eternities no gleam
  Of revelation sheds a ray of light ;
But where pale science throws at times a beam
  To guide the explorer's weary feet aright
Toward those caverned vaults with buried keys,
Where nature locks from man her mysteries.

158.

The innovator, the discoverer and
  The scientist, inventor, infidel, et al.,
Are the disturbers of the peaceful land—
  Are shaking our religions to their fall ;
So armed must be the governmental hand
  With javelin, as was the hand of Saul,
And it must smite, nor miss, as did the king
When David dodged aside with dexterous spring.

159.

Our land is ravaged by the fiend discord,
  Our laborers are idle through invention ;
It is not any more, "Thus saith the lord,"
  But what resolved this or last week's convention ;
Strikes and demands bring labor no reward ;
  Fresh patentees are ever in contention ;
A man fears to keep sober or get "tight,"
Lest he infringe some recent patent right.

160.

"Doubts" are the fellows that beget machines
  That do the work of forty pair of hands,
And thus enable owners, by their means,
  To run their shops, or mills, or till their lands
Without the laborer; hence his pork and beans,
  Or bread, which by his maker's own commands
He was to eat in toil and sweat of brow,
He can't come at, nor earn, nor get nohow.

161.

And this comes of the skeptic, who looks on
  And "doubts" if ancient methods are perfection,
And, without asking Jesus or St. John,
  Begins to project, after some reflection;
He works till midnight, and is up at dawn;
  He works in secret to avoid detection;
He gets a model, then assumes the role
Of an inventor, and—condemn his soul!

162.

You must excuse me for blaspheming thus,
  But honest gorge has no recourse but that;
All things in use has the inventing "cuss"
  Dam'd with a patent or a caveat;
This very pencil making here a fuss,
  The rack near by on which I hang my hat;—
All things about us, whether new or old,
Are clutched in the vile patentee's dead hold.

163.

But, after all, inventions, I concede,
  Or some of them, are useful to the race;
Some of the more destructive ones we feed
  With hostile christians, slaughtered face to face;
When population gains too fast on feed,
  This rapid killing, through infinite grace,
Is quite a blessing, and most honors fall
On the machine that kills the most, or all.

164.

But we believers, understand it well,
  Are sole inventors of destructive ram,
Torpedo, rifle, mammoth shot and shell;—
  The skeptic's turn is more for cog and cam;
At labor saving, the vile infidel,
  And in belittling the Great I Am,
By theories that put a lying face
Upon his "word,"—the heathen finds solace.

165.

For this we would suppress him ; and this brings
  Us back to the great problem of wise laws,
Claiming divinity for priests and kings,
  And putting Jehovah back where erst he was,
Above all statues, where, beneath his wings,
  All would be forced to worship, or show cause
Why they should not be burnt or starved to death,
Or otherwise yield up their useless breath.

166.

We ask, nor will evasion give content,
  For if it is not so we want it known,—
We ask, Is ours a christian government?
  Are god's decrees superior to our own ?
If not, why on thanksgiving day are sent
  The nation's prayers up to the great white throne,
By proclamation and much sound of gongs,
With savory dishes and some sacred songs?

167.

It is as christian, or with false pretense
  Our nation calls officially on Christ,
Say once a year, unless there's pestilence,
  Or drouth,—or bugs or hoppers need a hoist,
When proclamation of the president's,
  With piety and meekness duly spiced,
Sets forth that drouth, and bug, and hopper-grass,
Are but amenable to prayer en mass.

168.

And so, admitting heaven's ways inscrutable,
  The president selects a special day,
(The governors fall in, as being dut'able,)
  For the whole nation to fall down and pray,
(God's power to grant the prayer being indisputable,)
  That god will make the "'tater" bugs go 'way,
Break up the drouth, or stay the pestilence,
And kill, or drive the pesky hoppers hence.

169.

And so in cases of extreme distress
  Our nation owns god's majesty and awe,
And prostrate on its knees, asks him to bless,
  Although ignoring him in national law ;
Which inconsistency is little less
  Than an insult to him from whom we draw
Our very breath ;—hence, tho he sees our need,
He mostly lets the pestilence proceed.

170.

For which we cannot blame him, for in fact,
  While we exclude him from the constitution,
It is unmanly to ask him to act
  Upon the hoppers, and for a solution
Or stay of epidemics, which attack
  And fill our land with death and destitution :
Hence that no prayers bring rain is no great wonder,
In long dry spells, tho there may be some thunder.

171.

And this exclusion of our blessed lord
  From proper recognition, statutory,
Is chargeable to men who drew the sword
  And battled Bull until his horns were gory ;
They beat King George, and then with some accord
  They robbed the god of battles of the glory ;
And in their laws, enacted subsequently,
They don't refer to him, even incidently.

172.

And worse: those ingrates, by Tom Paine befooled,
  Hurled the unheard-of heresy abroad
That power to rule comes from the people ruled,
  Nor is and never was a gift of god !
A doctrine monstrous to sovereigns schooled
  To govern by the ritual and the rod !—
The skeptic Paine this heresy contrived,
That power to govern man is man-derived.

173.

And thus our nation in its infancy
  Against the almighty raised its puny hand ;
For blows at kings and priests strike deity,
  And we who weigh these facts can understand
Why prayers from us are powerless, and why he
  With plague and pestilence doth scourge our land :
We wrest our government from his directions,
And put our trust in lectures and elections.

174.

And yet aside from statute and decree,
  We're a god-worshiping, god-fearing nation ;
God's "word" is found in every "famile,"
  And school-house, court and hall of legislation ;—
God's costly temples from taxation free,
  As are his priests from useful avocation,
And half our people's time and earnings go
To god and church and priest, as facts will show.

175.

But these are infidel assertions, and
   You'll make allowance in accepting them ;
All "praise" of god, as we well understand,
   The hated infidels scorn and condemn,
But they pay their pro rata cash in hand
   For every sermon, song and prayer—ahem !—
And this is right when rightly understood,
   For wicked folk should help support the good.

176.

But we want laws a little more direct,
   For payment now is only incidental ;
We want it so that church-men can collect
   Their tenth from all, like any other rental ;
No less than this can clergymen expect,
   And that it pass in statutes fundamental ;
For those who take charge of the public morals,
Should be paid legally and without quarrels.

177.

They should be paid by law—not left to beg,
   And pass the hat on lord's day for collection ;—
Should have the tenth potato, chicken, egg,
   And the tenth quart of wine, gin and confection ;
And the tenth bushel, ton, and quarter section,—
   From this "posish" we will not move a peg,—
The church should have the tenth of all production,
Tho it engender rows and general "ruction."

178.

For 'tis no trifling thing to watch and guard
   The public morals and maintain propriety,
In every walk of life, and labor hard
   To weed the unbeliever from society ;
Blaspheming, sabbath-breaking to retard,
   Immoral theaters, known as "variety,"
Immoral dances, circuses to smash,
And guard the public mails from obscene trash.

179.

Indeed the world would quickly run to riot,
   Debauchery and wickedness most foul,
But for our savior's everlasting fiat,
   That fixed a brake in crucifix and cowl ;
Take off the church restraint one day and try it !
   Why satan would raid through our ranks and howl,
And blood would flow in every street and gutter,
And horrors happen that no tongue could utter.

180.

But by the gospel of the blessed savior,
　　Preached from a million altars day and night,
The wicked are kept on their good behavior,
　　And satan is supprest almost, or quite ;
'Tis true he makes demoniac endeavor
　　To put the preachers and the popes to flight,
And it takes billions of the loudest prayers
To drive him daily, hourly, to his lairs :

181.

For he whips out whenever there's a lull,
　　And raids society with fell intent,
Goading even priests to battle, fist and skull,
　　And in a twinkling doing such devilment,
That gospel weapons, if the least bit dull,
　　Fail to affright him from his horrid bent ;
So it is absolutely necessary
To keep the hosts of Zion armed and wary,

182.

And wide awake, for like the "son of man,"
　　Satan comes in an hour ye think not of ;
With an unseen yet soul-devouring clan—
　　(O sinner, don't thus turn your nose "aloff,")
The priest with holy water in a pan—
　　(O infidel, poor infidel ! don't scoff !)
Appears and sprinkles on the imps this fluid,
Which makes 'em fly as if they were pursu-ed.

183.

For fluid thus supremely efficacious,
　　We can afford to pay a monstrous price ;
This world of ours, so lovely, grand and spacious,
　　With satan out, would be a paradise ;
But he's so cautious and so contumacious
　*That holy water, with much church device,
Although it frights and checks and holds at bay,
Fails to destroy or fright him clear away.

184.

Hence at a glance we comprehend the need
　　Of constantly maintaining church and priest,—
The soldiers of the cross to clothe and feed,
　　And prosecute the war north, south, west, east.
The skeptic must, though grudgingly, concede
　　The church worth half our revenues, at least,
And we ask but the tenth, where half is owed,
For the tremendous benefits bestowed !

185.

There is no good that is not church-begotten ;
  The several virtues rise in church and creed ;
Outside of church, society is rotten ;
  The gospel is our chief, our only need :
We put upon the stand good Brother Cotton,
  A valued witness, as we all concéde,
The truth of these averments to attest,
And prove the infidel a hated pest.

186.

For Brother Cotton is an excellent hater,
  He gives the scoffing infidel no quarter,
And other ministers, some less, some greater,
  Would take the stand if we should say they "orter,"
And swear by their good book and their creator
  That earth has nothing good that wasn't brought her
With sacrificial blood by Pilate spilt,
Which brought all grace, and takes away all guilt.

187.

Our christian civilization has been won
  By spreading gospel tidings far and wide ;
The affecting tale that god had once a son,
  Which son by Jewish hands was crucified,
Has caused the tears from million eyes to run,
  Reclaimed the savage—this is not denied—
And gave us carts, plows, scythes, and hoes and axes,
And brought, we must admit, our tithes and taxes.

188.

With whisky and tobacco,—gaming cards?
  Well, these all follow in the gospel wake,
And something worse than these—the rhyming bards !
  The gospel, too, gave us the fiery lake,
But this invention no man now regards,
  Though it was long the minister's "fat take."
But I am off—I want to make the exposure
That no good fruit grows out of church enclosure.

189.

All this, however, the base infidel denies,
  Nor can we wonder when we once reflect—
Can there be truth in him who shuts his eyes
  To revelation, and who dares neglect
His christian duties ?—Who re-crucifies
  Our blessed savior—daring to reject
The preached gospel and the precious gore
Shed on the cross that sin might be no more ?

190.

Can we respect the skeptic who pretends
    He can't believe a son was his own father,
Or vice versa, for redeeming ends,
    When scripture says *'tis so ?*—or rather,
Are we not bound to see that he *ascends ?*—
    Had we not ought to mask ourselves and gather
About his house at deadly mid of night,
And fix his neck in a strong rope's dead bight ?

191.

Proscribe we may, but 'tis no longer legal
    To pinch, imprison, stab, or skin or burn him :
No saucier fellow marched and "fit mit Siegle,"
    So Christ upon the cross does not concern him :—
A cawing crow, that jeers the soaring eagle,
    That from its dizzy height may scarce discern him,
A buzzard, flopping round the christian flock,
That they may not molest, nor rout, nor rock !

192.

O there is comfort in the contemplation
    Of endless torment for the wicked man ;
He scoffs at Jesus and rejects salvation
    Upon the savior's blood atoning plan :
And yet Bob Ingersoll, with much oration,
    Will rob us of this comfort, if he can,
And give us not a thing in place of it ;
Therefore we want his horns hauled in a bit.

193.

Men who deny the bible, have they rights?
    May we not, for the good of god and man,
Remove them, when the lord removes his lights ?—
    May christian men not kill them, if they can ?
The wolf, the lion, the mad dog that bites,
    Have stronger claims upon our mercy than
The impious wretch that scoffs at holy writ,
Or the true creeds engrafted upon it.

194.

I say true creeds, and by true creeds I mean
    Those that enjoin faith, prayer and chant of psalm
As the chief christian duties—make you lean
    Upon dear Jesus, hoping he will damn
Those who deny him, but yet still will screen.
    Even murderers owning up that he's the lamb
That taketh sin away—whose blood was shed,
And who still liveth though reported dead.

195.

We hold that murderers, who believe and pray,
  Are innocent as babes compared to those
Who, like curs'd Judas, our dear lord betray ;
  They may be good and moral, but are foes
If they deny the Christ ; and christians may
  Lay snares for them and fill their lives with woes :—
May lie about and rob them—'tis no sin :
All's fair that's needful for our lord to win.

196.

Thus thinks brave Anthony, the christian's friend ;
  When in pursuit of the curs'd infidel,
He spares no measures needful to the end,
  Which is to cage the wicked in a cell :
His letters of decoy we can commend,
  Likewise the schemes he understands so well,
To tempt the unwary into overt acts,
Then seize and charge them home with stubborn facts:

197.

Because the ends to be attained are great—
  The infidel to trap and bring to grief ;
The cause of Christ to avenge and vindicate,
  Which justifies the Y. M. C. A. chief,
Armed as he is with powers of church and state,
  To play the sneak, the spy, the assassin,—thief,
Or aught besides best fitted to deceive,
And cause the heathen to disgorge and grieve.

198.

And as the agent of the vice society,
  Vice he may use to track and punish vice—
May pay bad girls to strip—then with propriety
  March them to prison naked, in a trice,
Or loitering, scan their charms to full satiety,
  Then march them off, the naughty things, (but nice!)
And take them nude before the "jedge," because
To doff their robes outrages christian laws.

199.

The christian law may peep in ladies' rooms,
  If peradventure it leads to disclosure
Of what, from their pursuit, the law presumes,
  Some ladies make—of hidden charms exposure
To men not their own priests, nor even their grooms !—
  And pray, how is our Anthony to know sure
Of secret vices and forbidden joys ?—
·They drive him to disguises and decoys,

200.

And if for dollars fourteen he could hire
　　Five girls to play nude Eve for hours some three,
For him and friends, the wicked who admire
　　Such exhibitions, by like bribery,
Could be like served, and thus god's fearful ire
　　Be terribly aroused—Thus Anthony,
In ferreting out vice, god's wrath averts,
And the prerogatives of church asserts.

201.

And vice, that church and state would undermine,
　　Find's Tony's schemes as sly as snakes in grass :
He plays it on the heathen awful fine,
　　In various ways ; but we will let them pass,
For in our Tony church and state combine
　　To give the world assurance of an ass,
With knave enough thrown in to indicate
Foul conjugation of Dame Church with State.

202.

But this I say with no ill will for Tony,
　　But just to allay the roaring heathen's wrath,
Who lays about him, with cold eye and stony,
　　And with much logic and his sword of lath ;
Contesting, teasing—wanting testimony,
　　And trying to turn men from the beaten path
That leads the christian upward to his crown,
To follow him in unbelief and *down!*

203.

And as the average heathen hates oppression,
　　And interference meddlesome with freedom
Of press and speech, and will make no concession
　　Of rights he claims to have, (and seems to need 'em,)
To mail facilities—to his discression
　　Whether to work on holy days, or heed 'em,—
We have to curb him gently—give him rein,
Then lay with Anthony for him again.

204.

We have to treat him gingerly because
　.He seems exceedingly to multiply ;
He is more contumaccous than he was,
　　Claiming he can with true believers vie
In purity of life ;—he hoots at laws
　　That plant the gospel in our schools—and why ?
He knows the gospel, if it would abound,
Must be sown early in untilled ground.

205.

He multiplies apace, as I have said,
  And so must be a little bit placated ;
We find him even at the nation's head—
  In office everywhere, but not elated ;
He leads in our best colleges, whence spread
  Those scientific heresies so hated :
He almost owns the forum and tripod,
And thrives, for all I know, by grace of god.

206.

But I must hurry onward. I reveal
  A growing tendency toward verbosity,
Which may in time make the judicious squeal,
  And wish the bard shot hell-ward with velocity
Akin to lightning. And sometimes I feel
  That it were well to weave in some monstrosity,—
Some blood-and-thunder hero, broke from jails,
To lend a charm to my dull Tale of Tails.

207.

Because a tale of blood and savage deeds
  Has fascination for your modern lad :
He rolls and ruminates his cud and reads,
  And swears when grown he'll be as smart and bad ;
He'll be a foot-pad, herding with half-breeds ;—
  He'll steal a pistol—run away from "dad"—
He'll rob the stages and he'll wed a squaw :—
He'll be a frontier hero—an outlaw !

208.

A story with a streak of blood clear through it
  Amongst your christian youths finds eager buyers ;
They'll read if they must lie and hide to do it ;
  The more highwaymen, pirates, champion liars,—
The more outlawry there is added to it,
  The more it takes ; the public never tires
Of the sensational, of scandal, war—
It nurses all, but I know not what for.

209.

Your nice dime novel, your Police Gazette,
  And kindred literature our prisons fill,
Our gallowses supply with victims—whet
  The appetite for blood, adventure—kill
All taste for toil and useful knowledge—yet,
  Though these fictitious narratives distil
Their deadly poison like the upas tree,
They are not warred on by brave Anthony.

210.

For they fight not the church, nor are they lacking
In faith, and fear of god and heaven and hell;
Their heroes bold, while safes and men's heads cracking,
Find time to pray, and sometimes preach as well;
And when a train or frontier village sacking,
They spare the priest and church; and when farewell
They bid the priest, with neck in noose of rope,
They ascend to Abraham, whose arms are ope.

211.

Not so the infidel—the books he prints
Are of a scientific or religious cast;
The sex relations he must mouth and mince,
Or over-population give a blast;
Nay, even must throw out vague, mysterious hints
About destruction of the cytoblast,
And other wicked measures that defy
God's mandate to "increase and multiply."

212.

He takes the ground that the vain creature man
May frustrate god's best efforts to create
Twelve children through one pair, and says they can
Not care for one, much less for twelve or eight,
If very poor; and poor folks always pan
Much children to the mine, while oft the great
And rich are childless.—God, all-wise, decrees
The babes to those—the brains and bread to these!

213.

And then the skeptic's books are contraband,
Because he prates about effects prenatal;
He'd have perfected men, like stallions, stand,
While those with taint, inherited, deemed fatal
To healthy progeny, he'd have unmanned,
Or by some other method would abate all
Prolific commerce where defects are glaring—
An innovation most absurd and daring!

214.

But what can we expect of innovators
Who ask us to apply to human breeding
The rules that farmers, horsemen, speculators,
Observe in breeding pigs and colts,—in seeding,
Whereby the soundest corn and best "potaters"
Are carefully selected? Such rules heeding,
We might in time somewhat improve the race,
But at great cost of god's infinite grace.

215.

For god "makes" everything as it should be,
  And to pervert his will is rank offense;
He makes what's lovable and good, and he
  Makes many things which we, with our weak sense,
Can't see the sense in making—'specially
  The poisonous reptiles—the great fountain whence
The evil passions flow. Could not the infinite
Create a world with only goodness in it?

216.

A perfect god would make a perfect man,
  A god of justice make his creature just;
A god all-powerful would perfect his plan,
  And nothing to the chance of failure trust;
A god all goodness would not set the ban
  Of endless torture on his child of dust;
Nor would a god of peace have planted strife
In the chief creatures that he spoke to life.

217.

But thus to speak of god is to blaspheme,
  I must not criticise and carp and cavil;
I am myself not wicked, like I seem;
  I only o'er the skeptic's roadway travel;
I feed his spleen and smiles upon him beam,
  Then hoot him out with groan and gong and gavel!
I voice his argument until it shocks,
Then blow him up with batteries orthodox.

218.

He sees no sin in thwarting god's design—
  Perverting nature wickedly for years,
He's rooted out god's good old roach-backed swine,
  And giv'n us Poland-Chinas and Berkshires!
And the descendants of Pharaoh's lean kine
  Has he remodeled into Devon steers!—
Thus mocking god and proving him unwise!
Improving on his work before men's eyes!

219.

And so with chickens, ducks, dogs, sheep and "hosses"—
  They're scarce the creatures that the lord created;
By intermingling and presumptuous crosses
  The sample pairs, with which the ark was freighted,
Have lost identity.—God's work man bosses!—
  The dog has keener scent, the horse is gaited,
The sheep has finer wool—this is the excuse
For tampering with god's work; but 'tis no use!

220.

God's vengeance never sleeps—a jealous god—
  He has a patent right on every creature;
Aware of this, man, insolent, unawed,
  Goes on remodeling—changing form and feature;
His imitations are produced by fraud—
  God is the original maker, moulder, teacher.
Man's puny touch no tint adds to the rose—
No added beauty to heaven's arched bows!

221.

Man calls this thwarting of god's purpose science;
  He reasons out results as he proceeds;
He watches nature's methods—his reliance
  Is in his power, as he perceives his needs,
To rally nature's forces, through appliance—
  Quick telegraph—the steam engine which speeds
The commerce of the world—God's elements
Enslaved to work machines that man invents!

222.

Water was made by god for men to drink,
  To put out fires, to wash in and to use
In floating ships; and likewise, come to think,
  In sprinkling and immersion.—We abuse
The bounty of our maker when we wink
  At making steam by boiling it in flues!
'Tis a misuse of god's material, hence
The bursting boilers, we call accidents!

223.

God suffers no infringement on his rights
  Without avenging it four thousand fold;
In scripture are his land-marks and his lights,
  Revealed by him to righteous men of old;
The earth is fixed, he thundered from heaven's heights,
  Yet skeptics later dared to say it rolled!
But lo! how quick god's vengeance overtakes
And burns to death the rogues, chained up to stakes!

224.

One wretched reprobate, Galileo,
  Once wickedly be-crazed good christian pates:
God's awful word he tried to overthrow!
  Said he, "The world is round and it rotates!"
But god brought him most suddenly to woe!
  Glad was he to kneel down to the prelates
And there recant; (contrition god approves;)
But rising, treacherously he lisped—"It moves!"

225.

God did not hear the horrible remark,
  For it was whispered slyly to a friend ;
But had he heard and struck him stiff and stark,
  There the vile heresy might have bad end ;
As it turned out this scoffer's flickering spark
  Grew to a fire, whose flames yet still ascend,
And light the skeptics, (scientists they're called,)
Through haunts where god's true word is overhauled !

226.

Aye, and disputed, criticised and scanned
  By rogues all asses saving length of ears !
They peck at rocks and talk of stratas, and
  Rise up and swear that god's six thousand years
Are not enough—that years as grains of sand
  Have been as numerous, (as to them appears
The evidence of rocks,) our globe to grow,
As if they more than the almighty know !

227.

And the philosophers ! god save the mark !
  Have robbed even christian people of their wits,
Till some doubt Jonah, others Noah's ark !
  While here and there a christian half admits
The earth a sphere !—bewildered—mad, mad, stark !
  But, thank the lord, the holy ghost still flits
Before the eyes of the great gospel host,
And shuts out heresy, I may say almost.

228.

What need man know, except that Christ was god,
  And died that we might not be cast in hell ?
Why search out paths save those our fathers trod ?
  They served our sires and why not us as well ?
To bruise the flesh and to embrace heaven's rod
  That scourges to the bone, is to excel
In christian work.—A wilderness is earth,
A transient state is life, and death our birth.

229.

Earth is not man's abiding place—O no !
  God puts him here but for a little season ;
Dark is the vale !—we work our way in woe !
  Faith is our guiding star—stop not to reason !
It is an ignis-fatuus blinding so,
  That following it, we see not our rank treason
Against the son of "man," till through the mire
We sink ! (O, horrible !) into hell-fire !

230.

Where there is wailing, wailing, wailing, wailing,
  And gnashing, gnashing, gnashing of the teeth !
Children a span in length—the mother hailing
  The husband up in heaven, who when he seeth,
He glorifies the lamb—his sight regaling
  Upon her horrid tortures down beneath;
He cries, "O glory ! glory !—justice, wife !
You joined another church than mine in life !"

231.

O what sweet music to the parent's ears—
  He sits by god and hears his children shriek,
He sees the flames wrap round the little dears !
  Midst cries and moanings, pitious, feeble, weak !—
These sights and sounds for endless, endless years,
  Make him love god the more, who needs must wreak
His dreadful vengeance on this son, this daughter,
Who were not sprinkled with his holy water !

232.

The torments of the damned ascend to heaven
  Forever, ever, ever, ever, ever ;
The saved and lost relate as one to 'leven ; `.
  The ten in hell can never, never, never
Have one brief moment's ease ; the one forgiven,
  No time from maddening ecstasies can sever :
His song is,—"Blessed, blessed, blessed lamb !—
O wondrous mercy—only ten you damn !

233.

And there were 'leven of us in the mine
  When it caved in. I and another one
Made our escape,—died without unction nine ;
  The tenth I stabbed ; for true love was it done ;
I craved his wife ; they hanged me with a line ;
  But I confessed the virgin, father, son ;
Took extreme unction, and I have my wings !
O, glory, glory to the king of kings !"

234.

In groping through this gloomy vale of tears,
  One joy remains—our Jesus we shall meet ;
And when we've sung his praise ten thousand years,
  We've just begun ; and wails—how sweet, how sweet,
From the 'leven tenths in torment, to our ears !
  And if the voice of once dear ones we greet,
Our praises ring the louder for their woes,
For love of god means hatred for his foes.

235.

This transient state! how full of woe and strife!
  Because to god our whole thoughts are not given;
There's nothing worth a moment's thought in life
  Save Jesus crucified and rest in heaven!　　•
Yet man takes joy in children, home and wife!
  In worldly pleasures!—O how man has striven
For wealth, for fame!—dross piled on top of dross!
And purchased at the soul's eternal loss!

236.

O in that day there will be wailing there!
  Hours given to pleasure here will there arise—
Hours that should have been given to groans and prayer—
  And give in evidence to our surprise!
The awful judge will say—"Depart! how dare
  You who loved earthly pleasure meet my eyes!—
You gave to wife, home, country, children dear,
Love due alone to me!—depart from here!

237.

I am a jealous god—my vengeance sleeps
  Not for a moment—whoso loveth me
Must hate the world—its creatures, golden heaps—
  Must make his earth life wretched as can be!—
By nature man's depraved: the heart that leaps
  With earth delight is daring deity!
All earthly loves and yearnings of the heart,
Must be suppressed!—Depart, ye curs'd—depart!"

238.

And this is why god often takes away
  Our little children, dearer than our sight;
He's jealous of them, for he sees that they
  Are robbing him of love that is his right!
So when they're gone, like buds and birds of May,
  And winter's frost our tender heart-flowers blight,
He thinks a closer walk with him we'll seek,
And love him better—be subdued and meek!

239.

This is so natural! How our hearts expand
  With love for god who lays our darlings low!
How meekly we bow down and kiss the hand
  Whose owner we besought to spare the blow!
Yet infidels, accurs'd, can't understand
  That god does this because he loves us so!
And wants to wean our thoughts from earthly ties,
And fit us for our proper sphere—the skies!

240.

Man's great mistake is that he deems the earth
　His native sphere—its beauties worth the seeing;
Its pleasures proper—harmless joy and mirth!—
　When he should live and move and have his being
As if this world were not:—his second birth
　Arrives full soon, which liberating, freeing
His spirit from its shell, he then assumes
A viewless role—mayhap in wings and plumes.

241.

Man's only business here is to prepare
　Himself, his soul for the celestial place
That waits the just; and O, he doesn't dare
　To trifle with the overtures of grace!
Where'er he moves is set for him a snare
　And satan meets him hourly face to face!
Beset on all sides, tripped at every turn,
His only safety is to pray and mourn!

242.

No wonder then the god-man sobs and moans,
　And from his pulpit wrings his hands and cries!
He hears loud guffaws where there should be groans,
　And for hosannas, wild hilarities!
O, how it grieves him that old satan owns
　The joyous throngs he warns with weeping eyes!
O, dreadful, dreadful, dreadful flame that rolls!
O, precious, precious, precious, precious souls!

243.

In agony of soul the good man raves—
　O, could he snatch from fire one brand to-night;—
One soul from out ten thousand he who saves
　Does more for god than he who steals his light
To 'luminate New York; presumptious knaves!
　Tom Edison! outlaw!—you have no sight!
And no New Yorker can obtain a wing,
Not even the plum'd and curled Conkling.

244.

All, all, New. Yorkers must go to the pit;
　Sam Tilden, Talmage, Conkling and John Kelly;
Train, Vanderbilt, Jay Gould—hold on a bit!—
　But 'tis no use—not one is good; to hell he
(I mean the lord) will Sodom sink; 'tis fit:
　In such a lot no one can see how well he
Could pick out lambs for glory—these abound
In Boston, though; which is their stamping ground.

245.

Culture is the strong hold of these, and clams
    In wholesome chowder, with choice apple "sass,"
Form the refining diet that becalms
    And gives such grace to Boston lad and lass;
So they mature in loveliness, like lambs,
    And grown, outsiders very much surpass:
In fact a man not Boston born or bred,
Can have but little culture in his head,

246.

Or little taste for beauty or for beans,
    For poetry, for sculpture, music, art,
Dry metaphysics, arid magazines,
    And lectures that for learning make you start
And dig your digits in your head for means
    To comprehend the culture, which, in part,
Is sounding words in most refined precision,
And in accord with Webster's last revision.

247.

Then famous for philosophy as food,
    Is Boston with her brood of worms called book,
With Monday lectures, little understood,
    By the great bioplastic oracle Joe Cook;
Or Joseph rather, for it is no "good good"
    To nickname mighty men, on whom we look
With awe and rev'rence:—but plain "Tom" and "Bob"
Applied to infidels with view to rob

248.

Those pests of dignity, or to express
    A wholesome christian scorn, may be excused:
And I must be excused when I digress,
    A privilege I have too much abused:
Revolving round the Hub!—(and who does less!)
    A fellow gets most awfully confused,
And mixes culture and memorial halls
With Cooks and clams and beans and codfish balls.

249.

Out in the Great West where democra-cy
    Doth much abound, and men are free as air,
Where platform, pulpit, press and pews are free,
    The rustic man of worth may stand as fair
As the more cultured; honest poverty
    Bars no man from preferment—none would dare
To draw the line upon the surging mass,
And form a favored or exclusive class.

250.

But in New England and the middle states
  The aristocratic spirit has full sway ;
The wealthy close their mansions and their gates,
  And keep the laboring classes well at bay ;
The places of amusement rent at rates
  That force the common herd to keep away :
Aye, even the houses of great josh exclude
And shut from gospel mush the multitude.

251.

So in the sunny south there's a divide :
  Between the ruling and the serving class,—
A gulf between them, very deep and wide ;
  The aristocratic few the wealth amass,
And live in splendor while the herds abide
  In squalid poverty ; but let that pass,
Because the civilization we so vaunt
O'erfeeds the few, the many leaves in want.

252.

This cannot well be otherwise, because
  The thoughtless herd will be improvident,
And should we equalize earth's goods by laws,
  Short-lived, indeed, would be the arbitrament ;
The few would gather in with greedy claws,
  The many empty out to the last cent,
And so the old conditions would recur,
Leaving triumphant fate sole arbiter.

253.

To pick out faults and to philosophize
  Is something easier than to point out cures
For ills and inequalities that rise
  Where'er we turn, and that poor flesh endures ;
But were all merciful, humane and wise,
  With that quick sense of justice which assures
Its rights to every creature, what a weight
Could be plucked from the heavy hand of fate.

254.

But I was speaking of the mighty west
  As being the home of true equality ;
Even ostlers here may say, "Pull down your vest,"
  To one worth millions, say some two or three ;
The rich are not "stuck up," and not depressed
  Is the poor man, however poor he be :
Not even a gov'nor would desire, or dares
To ape the aristocrat, or put on airs.

255.

There's small distinction or dividing line
　　Between the man that walks and him that rides ;
One goes to congress, one to a coal mine,
　　But there's no social barrier that divides ;
Your tailor even, (to make one man*takes}nine,)
　　Can move in toniest circles ; and besides,
Your barber has his credit in the bank,
And your coal-heaver with yourself takes rank !

256.

Attempts, however, although most ridiculous,
　　To form that aristocracy called cod—
Codfish I mean—are made, and serve to tickle us,
　　Who bear the burthens of the day and hod.—
Those would-be upper tens serve Mark, or Nicholas :
　　Are presbyterians mostly, fearing god,
And hating heretics ;—they would be grand,
But only with contempt and scorn are scanned

257.

By the brave multitude whose breath of scorn
　　Chills like the north wind on a wintry day,
And nips the miscreant, who, ignobly born,
　　Assumes superiority of mold and clay :
The largest ears at best are only corn,
　　Which aggregated nubbins far outweigh ;
Nor wealth nor rank superior worth impart—
He's the best man who has the biggest heart ;

258.

The deepest sympathy for others' grief ;
　　The broadest charity for men's mistakes ;
The readiest hand to give the poor relief ;
　　The sweetest balm for the poor heart that aches ;
No gaudy church official, gory chief,
　　Shines with such luster as the man who makes
Poor hearts oppressed with care with joy to leap,
And turns to laughing orbs the eyes that weep;

259.

To bring back color to the blanched cheek,
　　To put bright fires upon the poor man's hearth ;
To shelter the poor soul, who, worn and weak,
　　Has neither home nor friend upon the earth ;
The poor dumb creatures round us, patient, meek,
　　To care for tenderly—this is true worth,
And he whose nature prompts him to such deeds,
Is nature's nobleman, nor tinsel needs.

260.

An aristocracy where noble acts
  Would form the ennobling feature of the clan
(Which uppertendom lamentably lacks,)
  Would be an honor to developed man ;
For goodness should stand higher than the stacks
  Of bonds that make your nabob—higher than
The power and glamour of official place,
Which lends to aristocracy its charm and grace.

261.

False charm and falser grace, false tinsel,—toys
  For children's playthings all the outward show
That wealth parades, that emptiness employs,
  To daze the eyes of those it deems below
Itself in social rank.—Substantial joys
  From humbler rivulets and fountains flow :
Man's consciousness of having done his best
To be of use to man, brings sweetest rest.

262.

Who helps to bear his flagging fellow's load,
  Who helps the weaker in the unequal fight ;
Who spares the patient ox the lash and goad,
  Who freely gives to penury his mite ;
Who pays to tremulous age the homage owed ;
  To woman the respect that is her right ;
To tender infancy protecting care—
He is a true man and his worth will wear.

263.

And tho his walk be lowly and his purse
  Be scantily supplied, more worth is he
Than fifty who their selfish souls immerse
  In money-getting, granting grudgingly
To labor's hand its scanty wage, and worse—
  By combinations massing wealth, till we—
Till the great herd, who toil for daily bread,
Are stripped and starved down to the bone, and led

264.

A helpless, struggling mass, to pile up higher
  The heaps of gold for the monopolist :
To nothing more need the poor man aspire
  Than to work all the time and to exist ;
When health shall fail him and his limbs shall tire
  He promptly goes upon the pauper list,
His wife goes to the wash tub, and his brood
Of little children must be "skimped" for food.

275.

But mind, be it ethereal, fluid, flame,
  Or call it instinct, thought or intellect,
Its nature in all creatures is the same;
  From one great fount man and the small insect
Alike draw their supply. "What's in a name?—"
  Or why the horse's soul put out, reject,
While man's comes in for immortality,
When the two differ only in degree?

276.

But let us back to our ancestors rude,
  A long-tailed people, mischievous, gregarious;
A romping, chattering, shiftless multitude:
  Much given to cussedness and crooks as various
As floating clouds—thieves, liars, the whole brood,
  And living from paw to mouth, a life precarious;
Recording nothing—taking no note of time
And, thank the lord, not given to rum nor rhyme!

277.

Why I say thank the lord, you'll wonder much,
  Because the good set me a skeptic down,
Who would not anything religious touch,
  Nor thank the lord, but pay him with a frown;
But you'll not wonder why a bard, with such
  A lack of rhyming talent and renown,
Should thank the lord his grand sires did not rhyme,
For had they done so they'd have beat'n his time!

278.

But now have at my story—hang the luck!
  I want to tell it while I've reputation,
And ere the reader tires with common truck,
  And thinks he'll never get my revelation:
The fact is, fifty times have I been "stuck,"
  When on the eve of making a sensation,
And to oblige the rhyme have trimmed my sail
And made a failure,—as right here I fail.

279.

But 'spite of failures, I'll fight nobly on,
  As one with but one idea always fights,
Till his opponents are all dead and gone,
  Or come to see his hobby in his lights.—
Our sires were wont to meet on the green lawn,
  And there discuss their acorns, rats and rights;—
And the tail question had assumed a phaze,
That did all classes quite convulse and craze.

280.

The people were unequally divided ;
  The masses clamored to retain the tail;
But some progressives, who had mostly guided,
  Plead for reform and lopping by wholesale ;
They held themselves superior, and provided
  Their tails were off, they said they could not fail,
By standing upright, with improved posterior,
To show all other beasts a far superior.

281.

And then they could look down with quiet scorn
  Upon the cows, the 'coons, the cats, the skunks ;
And though the rat, the root and the acorn
  Still formed their food, in caves they could make bunks,
And not like owls the limbs of trees adorn ;
  Their friends, the elephants, with tails and trunks,
Would much admire them, standing up erect ;
And homage from all beasts they might expect.

282.

By standing up and walking they would find
  Their neighbors looking on with awe and fear,
When they perceived not sticking out behind
  The same old tail late so conspicuous here ;
They'd soon be looked on as a nobler kind
  Of beings from some other clime or sphere :
Then some reformer, trained up for a model,
Would strut before the crowd with duck-like waddle ;

283.

When jeers and shouts would greet him : so to-day,
  A woman comes in bloomers on the street,
The shallow snicker, and in some dismay,
  The deep make quite precipitate retreat :—
Still innovators have to fight their way,
  And all their life-time may incur defeat ;
But saviors of the race, the seed they sow
In ages still remote will sprout and grow.

284.

The reformers being few were "overslaughed ;"
  They taught by precept more than by example,
Until by accident a noted bawd,
  Lost her appendage—one superb and ample :
She moped and hid herself till healed,—'twas fraud,
  But her sole chance was to set up as sample
Of the gay future female and to lead
A new departure, prompted by her need.

285.

So boldly came she out upon the green,
  And on her hind legs moved with mincing wiggle,
Much like the maidens of our day, I ween ;—
  And the male fogies ranged in groups to giggle!
The male reformers waddled with their queen,
  Hoping by this performance to inveigle
The females of their race in the new fashion,
Which at that time there was no fame nor cash in.

286.

And to say truth—I often wonder why
  I am so like our noble Washington :
I feel inclined to, but I cannot lie.—
  To say the truth, our mothers, every one,
Looked on this ambling bawd with envious eye ;
  And right here was the great reform begun ;
Back to this point can evolution trace
The work that brought a tailless, two-legged race.

287.

And so you see the women were to blame,
  As some galloot-made Adam say of Eve,
Some myriad ages later.—'Tis a shame
  To blame them for our woes, but I believe,
In justice to ourselves, we men must claim
  That women keep us back—that they deceive,
Are slaves to fashion, frivolous, vain and fickle,
Lead us astray and cost us "heap" of nickle.

288.

Our great-grandmothers, seeing this lady prance,
  And look so neat and trim, with cavaliers gay
Upon her person meek attendance dance,
  Resolved to adopt the fashion, right away ;—
A gay courtesan once, perhaps of France,
  Was seized with swelling that she could not stay ;
Then in great hoops and haystack skirts she wallowed,
A fashion that all women quickly followed.

289.

This folly was the rage for many a year,
  And skirts grew steadily from big to bigger,
Until at last the ladies came to hear
  The secret of the fashion !—what a figure
They had been cutting !—but with many a tear,
  Off went the hogshead hoops, and then to rig her,
(Your wife, I mean,) took yards some thirty less
Than formerly she bought to make a dress.

290.

But our grand-dames for fashion staked their all,
   Their caudles once cut off came not again;
But let a woman once resolve to fall,
   And fall she will, nor stop for shame nor pain.
They met pursuant to a secret call:
   They twisted off each other's tails.—I fain
For woman's sake this history would suppress,
But truth is truth, and history'll have no less.

291.

They were discovered, and the old fogy gents
   Rushed in to stop the havoc, which they did,
When those already shorn skedaddled hence,
   And in the bushes their maimed bodies hid.
The fogies, terrified and robbed of sense,
   Gathered their children and their wives and bid
A hasty farewell to the reforming clime:
And types of these are monkeys of our time.

292.

Great was the exodus, a few remained;
   The women mostly were inclined to stay;
But their rude masters easily maintained
   Their ownership in these, and so away,
Like Moses on his march, they went and gained,
   As he did not, a country wherein they
Would not be bothered with the curs'd reformers,
The innovators, stump-speakers and stormers.

293.

All males suspect of taint were left behind,
   While all the females and their young were pressed,
Except some ladies of superior mind,
   Whose hiding places could not even be guessed;
These had determined to remain and find
   What came of the new fashion; therefore lest
They should be kidnapped, in the general scare,
They hid themselves with most deliberate care.

294.

And now the innovators, left alone,
   Crept from their holes to view the situation;
The maimed girls came forth, with sob and moan,
   While those still whole went through the operation;
Then the reforming gents, with gasp and groan,
   Wrenched off each other's tails—but O, creation!
How they did monkey round—half dead, half glad!
It hurt the girls, they said, not half so bad!

295.

Meantime the lady who the style had started
   Laid back and roared with laughter : she was well :
The way that she and her appendage parted,
   Now that the tails were all off, she would tell ;
Her tail was bitten off, and heavy-hearted
   Did she resign it.   From a limb she fell ;
An alligator (how that poor man squeals !)
Took off her tail, and she took to her heels !

296.

"And didn't you have it cut off for reform ?"
   The sufferers cried in chorus, looking wild !
"And didn't you do it for fashion and to storm
   The castles of old fogies ?"—and she smiled !
"Alas," they said, "our bleeding tails, yet warm,
   Reproach us here !   O, we have been beguiled !
We've carried out what was our firm intention,
But acted under strange misapprehension."

297.

Time passed away, and all the wounds were healed,
   And the reformers met to count their noses :
Their numbers were but few, but wide the field ;
   They chose the bawdy woman for their Moses ;
Though by deception she'd brought them to yield,
   They held that great reform oft pre-supposes,—
In fact requires to put it safely through,
Much crooked work and some deception, too.

298.

They had no children, and the score of men
   Divided up the women, giving each
Some dozen wives, and this disposed of, then
   They organized a school designed to teach
The upright method of progression, when
   It was resolved that it should be a breach
Of genteel manners to walk on all four,
Which practice must be stopped, nor thought of more.

299.

And as to children, it was here decreed,
   That if they came with tails, when ten days old
These should be twisted off, and thus the breed
   Would merge at last into a finer mould ;
As generations others should succeed,
   The improvement but the future could unfold :
And this progressive process being maintained,
Soon but a rudimentary tail remained.

And upright walked our sires with noble shape,
    And language with development evolved :
Thus we have Man from the primordial Ape ;
    The question of absorbing interest solved ;
Should one dispute, his neck I'll seize the nape,
    For my veracity is here involved,
And of our race, its progress and career,
I may some day say more, but rest we here.

SEYMOUR, IND., Feb. 3, 1881.—In the 105th year of American Independence.